Voting with Mommy

Written by
Jocelyn Yow

Illustrated by
Bonnie Lemaire

Halo
PUBLISHING
INTERNATIONAL

Halo Publishing International
7550 WIH-10 #800, PMB 2069,
San Antonio, TX 78229

First Edition, August 2024
ISBN: 978-1-63765-642-6
Library of Congress Control Number: 2024912404

Halo Publishing International is a self-publishing company that publishes adult fiction and non-fiction, children's literature, self-help, spiritual, and faith-based books. Do you have a book idea you would like us to consider publishing? Please visit www.halopublishing.com for more information.

This book is dedicated to Kayden and all children—the leaders of tomorrow.

Plaza

Boutique

CITY HALL

FIRE DEPT.

VOTE MAYOR EMMA

VOTE EVA

VOTE MAYOR JEAN

VOTE CONGRESS SARAH

4

It is October. The leaves are falling, and the weather is getting cold.

Kayden and Emma are on their way home from school, but today the streets look a little bit different. Across town, there are lots of signs and banners.

"Mom! What do the signs say?" Kayden asks.

Mommy says, "It's election season. This fall, we get to vote for our mayor, school board members, and even our president!"

Kayden and Emma are curious, and they want to learn more about the upcoming election.

Mommy takes Kayden and Emma to a town hall meeting at the local library. They are introduced to the mayor and the other candidates running in the upcoming election.

"What exactly does a mayor do?" Kayden asks.

"Well, I do a lot of things! I oversee the city. I help make our neighborhood safer and our parks nicer," explains the Mayor.

"Even the parks?" Kayden's eyes widen in awe.

The mayor nods. "Elected officials make decisions that affect our daily lives, even our parks!"

Kayden eagerly tells the mayor that we need more parks and playgrounds in the city!

After the town hall meeting, everyone is hungry.

"I want pizza for dinner!" yells Kayden.

"But I want pasta," says Emma.

Mommy suggests, "Well, why don't we vote on what we want for dinner?"

Kayden votes for pizza, Emma votes for pasta, and Mommy votes for pasta.

Kayden is disappointed, but Mommy reminds him that voting helps us make fair decisions about what to do when there are disagreements.

And it is important that everyone honors the vote.

Together, they have pasta for dinner, and everyone goes home with a full belly.

CITY HALL

VOTE HERE

VOTE MAYOR EMMA

VOTE MAYOR OLIVIA

VOTE MAYOR JE...

...HIA

VOTE EVA

...gress ...AH

18

And when Election Day comes, Mommy walks
Kayden and Emma to City Hall to vote.
There is a long line of people!

Kayden, Emma, and Mommy wait patiently. When it is finally their turn, Mommy votes, and the poll workers hand Kayden and Emma a big "I Voted" sticker!

VOTE HERE

CITY HALL

VOTE MAYOR EMMA

VOTE MAYOR OLIVIA

VOTE → EVA

I VOTED

gress

RAH

22

As they walk out of City Hall, Mommy gives Kayden and Emma a big high five. With pride, Mommy whispers to them, "Your vote is very important, and your voice matters."

www.ingramcontent.com/pod-product-compliance
Lightning Source LLC
LaVergne TN
LVHW070839080426
835511LV00025B/3486